How to Make a Dress out of Silence

Janice Windle

First edition

ISBN: 978-1-907435-13-3

Published by Dempsey & Windle

Guildford

www.dempseyandwindle.co.uk

Contents

How to Make a Dress out of Silence

Take a yard of the quiet of a dawn
before the birds wake.

Use the sudden hush before a truth is spoken
and the breathless pause in the eye of a storm
to create a template for your bodice.

Be sure to calculate
the volume of the air held in place
by the lungs' alveoli, so that it stretches easily
across the depth and breadth of your chest.

Cut out the skirt from a length
of the boundless, soundless vacuum of space.

Now thread a hiatus with a sense of absence
and sew into one peace.

Try on the dress.
Listen…

In the Case of Butterflies

Scarce the swallowtail; no more the pale
the clouded yellow's beating wing
disturbs time's continuum.
The small brown shoemaker's
exotic. At last
the future's fixed.
Butterflies
grounded
pinned

The Sun's Mythology

The sun is not a person.
The sun does not remember
its past, does not mourn
its future as a shrunken dwarf;
does not care for its planets
or their inhabitants
though in some sense
the sun is probably their parent.
The sun does not worry
about what other stars may think
as it runs a path through the teeming universe.

The sun is not a god.
The sun does not have obligations
or responsibilities or guilt or pain;
the sun is not pleased, nor grateful,
nor joyful, nor sad, nor puzzled,
nor vicious, nor vengeful.

The sun is a ball of burning gas.
The sun does not put its hat on.
The sun does not come out to play.

Heatwave

Missing the runway by a country mile,
a dragonfly from the ancient age of insects
cruises over the fields, crashes through
the open window, blunders into our faces,
bats its huge fragile body against the walls
until a smothering towel gives it pause.
It whirrs back across the meadow,
heavy as a freighter.

Each morning we rise
with foreign insouciance, casting
a cursory glance at the unchanging sky,
sure of the beat of the sun but exhausted
by the heat of a sleepless night;
electric fans have vanished from the shops.

Standpipes are in place on the east coast;
the radio is scare-mongering
and making promises, the farmers
praying and making only hay;
the children playing in seas that never were
so crowded, in August before or after.

The end when it comes is not a bang.
Small clouds gathering on the parched horizon
the gradual slide into the habit of
carrying umbrellas.

Al Fresco

Bring me tomatoes glowing red
In clusters on the vine!
From their sunny garden bed
Bring me tomatoes glowing red;
Bring me olive oil and crusty bread!
Oh gardener, bring me wine!
Bring me tomatoes glowing red
In clusters on the vine.

When in Rome

There's a church on every corner of every Roman street
and a stall selling statuettes and guidebooks
and a beggar with a mobile, and a dog lies at his feet.

There's a businessman in pinstripes, quite effete
(but could he be the Mafia, a really evil crook?)
and a church on every corner of each street.

There's a long-haired dark-eyed girl whose face is very sweet
outside the ristorante with a very sweaty cook
and the beggar with a mobile and a dog beside his feet

while the beggars on their mobiles are sending out their tweets
about our foreign meanness, by their baleful looks,
outside all the churches on the corners of the streets.

We were looking for a pizza, wondering where to eat,
(the scooters roaring past us, and how the piazzas shook
like the beggar with his mobile and his dog down at his feet)

then we found the Colosseum and the Forum in our book
and Trajan's Column that was crowned with a big rook
near the churches on the corners of all the Roman streets
and the beggar with his mobile and the dog beside his feet.

Daybreak

The first crack widened outside the Co-op.
The first brick moved aside at midnight. Twirling,
the white shoot rose, thrust, swelled,
divided, stretched, pointing furled leaves
towards the dark sky. Green sapling skin
hardened, split, coarsened, forked, irresistible.
When the first soft pale branches appeared,
they were cupped palms, thumbs open
so that we could fly in and leave at will.
We brought the first grasses,
fine straws of hay, down, reeds,
as dawn striped the horizon.
At dawn the egg was laid,
gleaming pearl, silver, opal,
Now we wait for the nestling hope
to take flight in morning sun.

His Name

In a niche in a wall
in the roofless croft
down in the field by the stream
I found him, or maybe
he found me.
His fists were raised
to the sky,
his creased robe carved
from a big ox bone,
a furious frown on his tiny face,
and he lay in my palm and screamed.

And his voice in my head
said his name, his name,
though perhaps it was only the wind.
And the sedge grew through
the fallen walls and the broken stones
where he'd lain on the ledge
when the croft was home
to the masters he'd served long past.

I carried him home
for he gave me no choice
and his voice sounded loud in my head
but I dared not speak
the name he'd revealed

in the field where he'd lain so long.
I've scribed it in blood of a butchered ox
on a leaf that I've hid in a hazelnut shell
and the nut is safe
in the leather box that Grandad made
in the shape of a shoe, that walks in time
to the beat of the kitchen clock.

Nameless he sits on the shelf by the fire
and keeps the home from harm
and shrieks in a voice only I can hear
his name, his name, his name.

God in the House

What is the secret of my success?
Omnipotence helps, I guess.

Your competitors?

No, I don't want to comment on Lucifer Inc.,
though I read that our rivals are right in the pink.
A long time ago, the decision was made
and I guess they're still doing a pretty good trade.

Was the casting a problem?

Yes, the casting was difficult - field was quite small -
it was Adam or no-one set up for the Fall.
But Evie turned out to be rather a babe -
such a shame, that bad business later, with Abe.

My son? You mean was he a chip off the old block?
Ask one of those chaps who likes wearing a frock.
He don't take after me - a lot more pacific -
and apart from his blockbuster, not so prolific.

And the future?

What am I working on in the next year?

Maybe tone down the pleasures, jack up the fear.

What would I have chosen to do differently?

….. Maybe called it a day when I'd created trees.

OK folks – no more questions today – Busy schedule …
[God has left the building …..)

Beauty and the Beast

The most beautiful woman in the room placed her smoothly coiffed head carefully on one side, resting her cheek on a slender hand. She looked up from under long lashes, her violet eyes alive with sympathy and understanding.

"Of course," she murmured to the squat toad-like man whose hunched shoulder almost touched her elegant elbow at the dinner table, "I see your dilemma. But my husband would not allow it. He's looking at us now.

"Yes, I know, " she went on, "I did it for him and I could do it for you." Across the table the most beautiful man in the room glanced towards them.

"And remember," she continued, "looks are not everything, and that's all my talent extends to."

"Just one kiss," begged the hunchback.

The perfect mouth of her husband opened and he held up a warning hand.

"Ribbet ribbet ribbet," he croaked.

Painting the Wind

I'm sitting astride the equator.
Weather streams towards me
across the South China Sea.
The sea wall is racing from under my feet.
On my easel the wind is painting
the enormous sky, the ragged clouds.

Long after, in a suburban room
someone will remark, "That's Dymchurch,
isn't it?"

The Gardener and the Artist

The artist can see five lakes, three farms, a railway,
round-hunched hills, and torn banana leaves
outside the gate, near Mohammed's home.
Mohammed is the gardener, a quiet man.
He grows and tends hibiscus. It's his work
to sweep the fallen petals from the garden.

From her rooftop the artist looks beyond the garden,
paints landscape, and trains that rattle on their way.
Last month the lakes drained dry. Now as she works
the women fill their bellied water jars. The leaves
are rafts of green. She is childless, unloved by her man,
feels like an interloper in this country far from home.

Foreign to them, this place will never be their home.
Each morning as the gardener sweeps the garden
she sees her husband leave. He is a busy man.
He's driven to the teeming city. Not far away
the gardener has a family: the wife he leaves
each day is caring for his children as she works.

In the fields Mohammed leads a bony buffalo, works
the dusty land. This is no Eden, but his home,
where typhoons bend the palm trees' leathery leaves.
He labours on his farm and from the garden
he brings the artist flowers to paint. It's his way
of offering to help her as she works, this man

of another faith, a father, a handsome, sensual man.
She loves him, guiltily, thinks of him as she works.
When one day they hear they must go on their way,
leave this hilltop where she's tried to make a home,
she wanders sadly through the high-walled garden
and packs and cries the day before they leave.

Mohammed comes to say goodbye the morning that they leave,
brings flowers to her in the echoing house. He is a proud man
who bears this parting gift like treasure from the garden.
His eyes are warm, feet dusty from his gardening work.
Their gazes meet. She drops her eyes from his, wishes the home
she longs for could be here and not a continent away.

The moment hangs between them like the dust, all work
forgotten, until they step away, each back to their proper home:
she to another country, Mohammed back into the garden.

Dhaka Games (A Sequence)

1. Scrabble Tankas

They build words in turn
relate their differences
life is not their dream.
Scatter pieces, end the game.
Love, exit, both possible

Loyal to his needs
weeping for a child she pivots
between life and love.
In a maze, a mist, a dream,
never exit nor ask why

```
                    A DD    F A
          G H O U L  A          S
                O   R      I RK
              P I V O T        I
            L I FE          N O T
D          O        W        T A
R    W H Y  J    E D        O
E    E   A L O NE        B U N
A    A   L    I    P L E A S E
MI ST        N    I        B    V
        H              N        Y    E
MAZE     R I N G                R
     R      C                G
    Q U E S T            U
        D    E X C I T E
```

2. Scrabble

Each night they exchange words,
keep the score.
Tonight she starts: ALONE.
across it he plays LOYAL;
she adds WEEPING.
He begs WHY
and her reply is BABY.

He asks PLEASE;
she counters NEVER;
he mentions WEATHER;
her answer is a MIST;
he gives her RING:
but her retort is ICED;

he insists upon his QUEST;
she returns her DREAM;
he adds an L, an I, an F:
and parries: that is LIFE

And still the Z, the X, a V
are waiting on their wooden racks.

Perhaps to leave this MAZE he'll use the V
to make LOVE, block her urge to EXIT,
add C and E to that and maybe
tonight he'll scatter board and counters,
forget the Scrabble, play another game.

3. Dhaka Games

On the veranda
Ashok sets out the board
the two opposing chairs,
the gins and tonics
and withdraws discreetly
to do the washing up.
The hasty sunset dies.
Attracted by the little lamps
heavy beetles clatter to their deaths
against the metal screen.
Sahib and Memsahib
are playing their nightly game,
says Ashok to the cook.

Rajendra's impatient:
he too has games to play;
at the gate behind the kitchen
his lover waits.
Ashok sings to his wife
far away in Chittagong
and listens.

The signal comes at last.
He carries in the deferential drinks
and is dismissed.
He leaves them to their silent games.

Tattoos

In the sixties it was CND:
badge of belonging, them and us.
She saw the solemn pie-chart as an anxious face.
She etched it on her shoulder
and marched at Greenham.

In the seventies she fell in love.
A crimson heart stretched across her chest.
No name.
Its counterpart, torn,
seeping tears of blood,
came later. When she married
they said it was for money.

The eighties brought a flush
of dollar signs, fistfuls of cards,
sterling symbols rearing like vipers up her forearms.
On each ankle, chains of harsh blue ink.
Her wedding ring covered the celtic knot
encircling one finger.
L – O – V – E
defined her other knuckles.

When the marriage failed,
across her belly she created the Titanic,
broken, half-submerged in the ice
of their last years together,
but the century turned
and champagne bottles on her thighs
flexed and sparkled.

Now travel was her comfort:
across her back an ink tsunami threw
islands, palm trees, parrots, flowers
entwined with initials of new loves.
With the Mappa Mundi on her shoulder-blades
"Here Be Dragons". Serpents wreathed her spine.
Around her neck toothy demons struggled,
locked with angels chanting open-mouthed.

And so at last she got religion.
A crucifix was hammered on the surface
of the temple that was her body.
Its arms invaded hers.
Her spine stiffened with stylised wood-grain
and blood ran from the nails upon her feet.
Head shaven, she accommodated
the godhead's suffering;
the crown of thorns encircled both their brows.
At last, the canvas of her body was complete.

Dancer

centre stage spinning and dipping and splitting
a glittering atom the rhyming
of timing and sinew and muscle and rhythm
the possible pushed to the limit that's in it
transformed without mask or paraphernalia
no words no regalia no shadow of failure
he's joy and he's wonder
he's thunder and lightening
he's tightening a band on the pulse of the world
and the night is the howl of the dancer's delight
and the dancer is king the dancer is king

Spoons

In the warm kitchen
the sprouts bubble,
the tiny potatoes I scrubbed
in icy water
simmer under tipped lid,
the windows frost with steam;
Henry weaves his striped tail,
circles persuasively
expectantly.
My grandmother carves fat duck.

I set the table and feel important.
My grandfather pushes up striped sleeves
under his red armbands
and picks up a pair of spoons
in his veiny knobbled fingers.
Against the chattering tympany of simmering pans
he clatters and clacks metal on knee and bony elbow;
he's singing "Underneath the Arches"
to my wide-eyed stare.

I can't remember the taste of duck
but a taste of amazement lingers
that such music was created
that far-off Sunday
from such ordinary things.

Telling the Time

It's a perfectly normal day.
It must be after eight o'clock;
the sky is white and grey.
Lost in his bag of breakfast oats
the milkman's horse is standing
winking his sticky lugubrious eye.

He waits; this is pay-day:
the milkman knocks at every door;
white bottles stand on every step:
it must be Friday, sure.

It must be half-past eight:
housewives wave in curlers and scarves;
little girls hop and skip from gates
chanting spellings and twelve-times tables:
it must be nineteen fifty-four.

It must be nineteen fifty-four:
chanting spellings and twelve-times tables
little girls hop and skip from gates;
housewives wave in curlers and scarves:
it must be half-past eight.

It must be Friday, sure:
white bottles stand on every step;
the milkman knocks at every door:
he waits: this is pay-day,
winking his sticky lugubrious eye.

The milkman's horse is standing
lost in his bag of breakfast oats.
The sky is white and grey:
it must be after eight o'clock
on a perfectly normal day.

Oracle

Mrs Brown sticks her cigarette
into the half-empty coffee cup.
"Racing Demon out of Marathon
and Lucifer - twenty-five to one."
My mother pours tea for Mrs Brown.
"Going's soft" she frowns,
and bends again to read the tipster's runes.

"I better do the spare room today,"
says Mrs B. My mother murmurs,
"Billy Liar's looking good."
Silence falls. The busy clock recalls
Mrs B must go soon to the village tout:
selections must be made,
accumulators calculated.

My tip, Maiden's Prayer, whose dad is
Out for a Duck, his mother Princess Grace,
is good for a bob each way, my mother reckons.
They plot together on yellow slips.

Next day, "Go on, pick us another winner,"
say Mum and Mrs B, and I know
I'm an oracle; I can't go wrong, they say.

Longing to be Joan

And so to my blue chair with wings
to hold me safe and blinkered from the world:
I sink against the worn brocade
grasping my beloved who lives between
cheap red pasteboard covers and grins
above his rumpled collar, from line drawings
on thick pages. I'm in love all right.
Crikey, says Ginger, *ole Marky nearly caught us
that time*, and they're calling, searching for me
but I'm far away in middle England
between two world wars. Violet Elizabeth
is about to *thcream and thcream until she's thick*
and William is proving again
that he's the charismatic leader of the gang:
master problem solver, adventurer, fundraiser
and the only boy who can make me laugh aloud.
And that's how they find me.
Crumbs, says William. *Girls*, he says.
And I'm delightfully, unreasonably,
hopelessly in love.

In Grandmother's Footsteps

Stroke it
down like
this fifty times
each morning and
it will grow straight....
Grandmother's warning rang
in my growing ears. Bemused - the
implied criticism rendered the button
I used to take for granted into a feature
ripe for relabelling by canny bullies; the
slope of it ghosting in the corners of
my eyes redefined   as ski run,
piggy, pug, or, more kindly,
retroussé, for I never took
Gran's advice: after all, it
clearly hadn't worked for
her, I thought.

Unfinished

I'm waiting patiently for my tits to get finished.
Brigitte Bardot is beautiful, I think.
I saw her in a film wearing this fluffy pink
sweater with a tight belt. With awe
I saw clearly that *her* tits *are* finished. I know
Mum says that mine will grow. But I looked just now
and if anything they've diminished.

Ursula Andress
in a state of undress
was simply the best
because of her chest.

Sophia Loren
attracted most men
had a sultry expression
even with a dress on.

On the Shore

Three girls.
They play there:
swing on the rusted railing,
hand over hand over the shallow burn,
over the yellow current streaked from a pipe upstream.

There's a rail track:
real wagons labour along
between the quarry and the limekilns.
(Even then ragged robins grow boldly
between the grainy sleepers.)
They hail the impassive drivers,
unlatch the gate to wave the convoys through.

They are engineers in the silt:
they dam the delta
where warm sewage fans out
to meld with brackish Firth water.
They build their towers
of stones polished by the storms
in the unkindness of coastal breezes.
They top them with white quills
donated by gulls.

The lobed seaweed like salty grapes frightens them:
harbours the grotesque unknown;
waves like alien life in the high-tide pools.
Dried, beached, the weed
loses power. They snap its pods triumphantly.

Nearby, fifty years away,
a gray-haired woman turns from her memories.

*

Locked

In the days when we were a shared refuge
I tried to tell you how it was going to be:
the changing of the locks on our hearts;
the redirected, poorly translated mail,
illegibly transcribed by our suddenly
illiterate selves; I knew how it would be:
I was a daughter once.

Stopover in Algiers, 1953

Algiers was a melée of colour and darkness.
On the dock bales and stacks of crates
and ropes coiled like animals
awoke in sailors' hands, snaking
over Halloween apple debris
bobbing against the quay.

Little boys held out carved animals,
draped rugs and fringed scarves
to tempt my mother
They must have been
as old and young as I, but
I did not think this.
To me these children were not
fellow-children. They chattered strangely
as they were brushed away
by our soldier and we plunged

from glare to pungent dusky tunnels
through peeling arches, past tiled fountains,
beside walls hung with glittering
bazaar wares. Men swathed head to foot
knelt on patterned mats in dingy doorways
and in the deeps of their shops
brass glimmered, copper dishes chimed
thinly. Under our sandals the dust
rose and stung our English nostrils.

The city clattered, shouted, breathed out smells,

sang and wailed. In the evening, back
safe again in our temporary floating cells.
From the deck we looked at dwindling minarets
and knew our lives had regained order:
the dinner gong, the deck-quoits, swimming races,
children's games: the voyage went on.

Where are all the Boys?

Faces flicker on my internal screen
Where are all the boys I used to know?
they Valentino'd me in my imagination:
innocent, driven, each one one of a kind.

Where are all the boys I used to know?
Robin, Joseph, Sean and Pauly Begg:
innocent, driven, each one one of a kind;
more differences than similarities, it seemed.

Robin, Joseph, Sean and Pauly Begg
one velvet-dark, one loose as ginger string;
more differences than similarities it seemed:
when I was young each meeting was unique.

One velvet-dark, one loose as ginger string
and Paul the butcher-boy, where is he now?
When I was young each meeting was unique:
In love or out, men were a mystery.

And Paul the butcher boy, where is he now?
Red-faced, rotund, suffused with bad cholesterol?
In love or not, he's had his mystery
exposed by life's insistence to conform.

Red-faced, rotund, suffused with bad cholesterol,
I only meet such social stereotypes,
exposed to life's insistence to conform,
boys hidden in the roles they have put on.

So now I only meet with social stereotypes
(I now a lady of a certain age, with
more similarities than differences exposed it seems)
Where are all the boys that I once knew?

*

Where's Megan?

She's crying in the toilets again
because she doesn't want to see Nathan.
Her friends gather like magpies, her pain
like a seeping morsel on the M25.
Questions, guesses, suggestions, sympathy
run before her to lesson three: Art.
Megan's missed. The boy Megan kissed
sits in Maths, considering with his mates
the Chelsea v Man U match, ignorant of his fate.
Her friends can't wait: the news percolates
and Megan smiles again.

Add a Little Time

So much in nineteen fifty-six was mystery and initiation.
At eleven we were initiated into Domestic Science, for our
womanhood's sake. (We never thought of our mothers as
Domestic Scientists. Nor do I believe that my daughter
later regarded me as a Home Economist.) To giggling girls,
in plaits or solemn fringes, Domestic Science was a temple.

Miss Cavendish was high priestess. As acolytes we owed
obedience in her kitchen. Obedience entailed: the wearing
of strange headgear and aprons, both sewn the term before
in Needlework; the thorough washing of hands and dishcloths;
the provision of paper bags of ingredients and containers.

Disobedience was punished by exclusion from the mysteries,
including the making of rock-cakes. Which required:

the sifting of fluffy white flour into a china bowl;
the weighing out of grainy caster sugar; the precise disection
of a yellow slab of margarine; a cup of water set to hand.

Then the rubbing–in begins: the marge cut finer, finer, finer,
engulfed by flour and gritty sugar crystals, then delicately
manipulated, rolled each crumb between gentle fingertips.
A rhythm builds as our hands rise, fall, rise, fall,
showering crumbs like snow back into the bowl.

And now a peppering of cinnamon, a scattering of sultanas
and a libation poured drop by drop, the dough piled
in little heaps on greasy trays, offered up to the pre-heated

oven for transformation. The scent of cinnamon baking.

I was a forgetful child. I seldom remembered to bring
the headband and apron. I became adept at washing up,
cleaning tables, scraping pots. Only once I made rock-cakes.

Today I'm looking at the little apron and the headband
embroidered with my name, the one that hasn't changed.
My mother, who was far from being a scientist, an economist
or a priestess, saved them. I guess she loved me. We made
fairy cakes and scones, Victoria sponges, butterfly cakes,
crumbles, brandy snaps and once a Swiss Roll. We rubbed in
fat and flour, creamed butter till it was so light it might fly,
melted chocolate, chopped angelica, sprinkled hundreds
and thousands, dusted icing sugar in snowy drifts. And
we never wore uniforms in my mother's kitchen.

Diamond Jubilee

"Look at me," says Dad.
She's busy with her pink umbrella;
seahorses and fish swim round it.
It isn't raining yet.
"Smile", he says.
She puts the umbrella between her teeth,
gnaws and smiles through it.
"Here", says Mum, "wave your flag."
She waves a blur
and returns to her umbrella.
Mum waves the flag,
balancing her paper cup of railway tea
in her other hand.
"That's a good one," says Dad.
But here's the train, pausing in that
self-important way
before it releases its load.
We all file on,
the flag and the pink umbrella
furled. She will remember, later,
only the pink umbrella.

When is a sign not a sign?

We had fallen out.
All the signs were there:
the white-knuckle tension;
the restricted eye-contact;
the silence humming
below the car's engine.
You said, "You're speeding."
I was not so I didn't answer.
You said, "Keep to the left lane."
I was so I didn't answer.
Then the sign by the motorway said,
"Signs are not in use."
and when I said,"and ceci n'est pas une pipe"
you gave no sign of hearing me.
Signs were not in use.

boring are we there yet road signs bits of blue white lambs dragons in the sky that's a horse how many red cars an ambulance nee naw nee naw they're cross again he's not looking at her must be my fault I shouldn't ask if we're there the baby's asleep what am I supposed to do in the back here and no-one talking to me now they're not saying anything to each other I'm thirsty can't we stop there's a Little Chef sign no we've gone past it are we there yet Mum suddenly says something nesepasunpeep it sounds like and Dad says nothing but I can see he heard. I ask Mum what she means and she says it means she doesn't want to hear another peep out of me so I know she's cross with me as well as Dad so I keep quiet until I see the sign that says to the beach and the thin dark line that looked like a cloud becomes the sea and the sun comes out between the dragons and the lambs and the signs are that the day will get better after all.

Incident on the Road

He stopped the car. She said,
'Was that a fox?'
He opened the door and got out.
It was dark outside.
He saw a dog pinned
under the front wheels.
It was not dead.
He lifted it up and carried it
to the side of the road.

When he got into the car she said,
'Was it a fox? Was it dead?'
He told her it was a dog.
Outside, the dog howled.
She said, 'Maybe we should...'
He told her they were in a hurry.

He drove on, to the airport.
Four times during the holiday
she said, 'I wish we had...'
He said they had been in a hurry.

As they drove home from the airport
she suggested they stop
at the place where the dog had been.
He said nothing as they drove past the spot.

The End of an Affair

We drove north on a road
that struggled, shook free
of theodolites, ran,
full of gritty mischief,
in violent arabesques
alongside deserted lochs.
The sky frowned over
asperities of granite
thrown up in the calamity days.
Time threatened to liquefy,
pool, break like a tsunami
over our passive heads;
slippage would reveal the moments
when we could have spoken
but feared to rupture
the cooling crust of indifference.
We drove north like salmon
towards the place where "we" and "us'
were first conceived. By Ullapool
it was decided; in Oban we spoke the truth.
When we ran out of road
the break was sealed
and we were friends again.

The Bed-sitter

Sometimes when you pause, key poised,
before the panelled doors,
time pauses, shifts, quakes.
Footfalls on the stairs echo
from far off; the cheap pictures
on the flock-papered walls
shiver to an earlier trauma.

Insert the key: your room
is as you left it. The single bed,
the electric ring, the washbasin
with your prickly towel underneath,
all untouched. The muffled laughter,
the whispers, did not come from here.

Ambition

I want to do it all, I said, I want to travel:

I'll visit every country, every continent,

I'll travel by camel, by elephant, by rickshaw, by jet-ski,

by helicopter, by supersonic plane, by yacht, by train,

by balloon, by riding on the back of the dodo that I'll find

on my famous scientific expedition,

by arctic sled, by sedan chair, by submarine, by rocket

(but not on horseback or a bike because they frighten me.)

I'll be famous for my dancing, my painting, my gymnastics,

I'll be famous for inventing edible plastics, for my skill at quoits,

for my sexual exploits, for my piety, my escapology,

my tightrope walking, my fast talking in Swahili,

my play-writing, my copy-writing, my bull-fighting,

my politicking, my Fairisle knitting, my witticisms,

my literary criticisms, yes, I'll do it all, I said,

and did I?

No, I didn't.

Travelling

She was smirking in a convertible in Paris;
he was frowning in a street-car in Saigon.
She was beaming on a bendy bus in Blackpool;
he was scowling in a transit van in Tring.
She was laughing on a steamboat bound for Dixie;
he was tearful in an Amazon canoe.
She was chuckling on a Chattanooga choo-choo;
he was snarling in a box-car in Peru.
He was weeping on a liner bound for Sydney;
she was sorry on a lorry by Loch Lomond;
he was smiling on a bicycle in Iceland
she was glad to see him walking up her street.

Goat Boots

Ants' sandals, wasps' socks
underpants for cockroaches
Don't you think that insects
should be clothed and not go nude?

naked beetles long for berets
lizards need their scarves.
Toads like smart tuxedos –
they don't do things by halves.

Goat boots, hippos' hats,
cardigans for cattle,
hats with corks for spiders
to attract the fiies with rattles.

gloves for gerbils, skirts for cats,
ball-dresses for tigers,
moccasins for micro-hogs and wellies
for fish swimming in the River Niger.

Don't you think it would be nice
to help God's little creatures
by making see-through macs for mice
and bras for the anteaters?

Animal Psychology

Wanderlust is not uncommon among hamsters
since they first perfected travelling on wheels.
Schadenfreude is a trait that some rabbits - one in eight -
will admit to, with vicious little squeals.

Claustrophobia's a problem for the ferret -
for them, travelling in trousers makes them sick.
Hysteria is found in many moles underground
so they have to dig their tunnels very quick.

Glauckenstücke is what every goldfish feels when
it knows it has been revelling too much
in the sufferings of flatfish who are bullied by catfish
or the battered cod the cat won't even touch.

Aphasia can be fatal in a parrot
Dyspraxia affects one snake in three
Guinea pigs who can't relax get mild panic attacks
but respond quite well to water therapy.

Schadenfreude - taking pleasure in others' sufferings
Glauckenstücke - guilt abut taking pleasure in other's sufferings
Aphasia - speech disability
Dyspraxia - manual clumsiness

How do Automatic checkouts work?

Technology's a wondrous thing
It helps us check our shopping in
the automatic checkout.

Just wave an item at the glass -
a barcode striped like a beetle's ass
makes beetles in machine flip out.

They squeak at the right frequency
to activate a camera – send, you see,
an image of the barcode beaming out.

This pic's picked up in no time flat
by the team of high-level autistic geniuses that
work in the back room of the store; they work out

and type the price into a till
send it by email and soon it will
reach the machine where it is printed out.

Simple really. If only the beetles didn't keep getting overexcited
and demanding to see the store assistant's barcode as well.

Start living your Tomorrow from Today
(Thanks to Saga Magazine advertisements)

Cross your closest friends from your Christmas list
and write DEAD across their names.
Begin ordering all your food online
because you fear you may fall over
if you go shopping on foot.
If you go out, take a stick with you,
to trip up younger walkers.
Ignore people if they speak quietly and
tell them not to shout if they speak loudly.
Get a state-of-the-art hearing aid.
Don't wear it.
Fit a stair lift and ride up and down just for fun
(it's never been easier says Saga Magazine)
Move closer to your doctor's surgery.
Make a will and tell all your relatives
not to expect an inheritance
unless they visit you often,
with flowers and chocolates and wine on your birthdays.
Wear a support stocking and/or a truss
whether you need it or not.
Take a new driving test.
Fail it by driving the wrong way on roundabouts.
Remind any young people you meet that you've seen it all before.
Get a cat and overfeed it.
Ring radio shows to complain about
decimalization and the price of cat food.
Write poems about getting old.

Intelligent Spectacles

Peering left, squinting right
my spectacle-detector's made
to scuttle till within its sights
it has the glasses I've mislaid.

My lost spectacles unharmed
from backs of chairs and under books
hop upon their plastic arms;
their lenses glisten as they call:
"Look! O look! Please take us back!
We were not lost at all!"
And now I've all the specs I need
myopic, astigmatic, tortoiseshell,
wire-framed, frameless, sunglasses
or do I want to read?

But still they clatter goggling out,
lenses bug-eyed at the call;
and now I need another gismo
to find the cases for them all.

Only the Best

This would be no picnic, they told us:
no summer break, no round trip.

Frosted in the hold
we lay like monuments to ourselves,
the life-support cables dangling above,
ready for instant automatic connection
in the event of sudden temperature rise.
Spectroglass visors showed our mute faces,
the children clutching teddy-bears,
Buzz Lightyears, Barbies; our adult skulls
full of frozen thoughts and snapshots
of excited anticipation.

Did the ship drone? Hum? Roar?
Did it buck and yaw on astral winds,
dip into deep space troughs,
spiral dizzily through Saturn's rings
on the way out of the Sun's safe haven?

Only the distressed panels of its hull
gave us clues, as, unsteadily, we disembarked
on the arms of the welcome stewards.

Only the children were not sombre
when they saw the town.
They held up their teddies,
their Buzz Lightyears, their Barbies.
"Look!" they cried, as we surveyed

the Forth Bridge, towering next to
the Pyramids of Giza; the Amazon
lined with skyscrapers from Manhattan,;
the Sydney Opera House proudly
next to the Leaning Tower of Pisa.

We only imported the best, the biggest,
the steward said, and we stood there and wept
for our suburban streets.

*

Antigravity

The capacity to fly a kite
is inversely proportional
to a man's gravity.
His faith in the absurd is all
that lets him hear the words
of the birds cruising in the stratosphere.
His kite tugs the rational tether
that holds him to the earth's skin
until the string cuts wild arabesques
in clouds, brands his hands
with stripes of its will to freedom.
Hovering on roaring winds
the kite's frivolity.

I'm in Love with your Mandible, Darling

I'm in love with your mandible, darling:
it's the mandible of my ideal man;
masculinity sings from your symphysis
as it has since the world began.

Etched almost as deeply as Mitchum's,
your mental protuberance, square and fair,
(and your incisive fossa) are only enhanced
by your carefully managed facial hair.

Trimmed neatly along each ramus
and across your strong oblique line,
your beard traces clearly your mental tubercle;
your powerful platysma is highly defined.

I'm in love with your mandible, darling;
the reason I love it is this:
when we're face to face in a private place
I love when our mandibles kiss.

Brazen Hare is

a wooden coin
is the round night
is a painted window
is a hunched cottage
is a bland moon
is a twisted puppet
running along a whetted blade.

To my Lover Dónall (with apologies to Christopher Smart)

for firstly he maketh many quips and is tireless in his merriment
for secondly he never is weary of teasing and his puns are legion
for thirdly he utters haiku in the morning
for fourthly he speaks poems in the afternoon
for fifthly in the evening he speaks volumes
for sixthly he is generous with his praise, his books and his advice
for he distributes all these liberally
for he weareth odd socks and is unrepentant
for he weareth his Panama hat and careth not that its crown is broken
for he loves fry-ups
for his creation of fry-ups with a profusion of heat and oil
for his love of open cupboard doors
for his ability to stack almost all crockery in the house
into the kitchen sink
for his ingenuity in filling the dishwasher
for his rendering of pans richly coated and black
for his gifts of cups of tea at any hour of day or night
for his voice which is deep and sonorous when he is calm
and high and shrill if he is wronged
for his hair which is abundant and curled
for his hair is a source of wonderment
for his hair is titled Robert Plant by the young
for he is not proud except when others scorn him
for he is not scornful except when others are proud
for he offers his chest as a pillow
for he offers his hands to warm his wife's feet
for he carries the history of his ancestors in his head and can divulge it
for he carries the history of his loves in his heart
and can utter them in songs, and for that he loves me I love him.

Now that I'm Old

(To Jenny Joseph)

Now I'm an old woman I'm wearing purple
and straw hats whether it's sunny or not.
I'm spending my pension on holidays in hot places
and bikinis I shouldn't be seen in, and computers.

I've learnt about IClouds and Ipods and IPads
I buy cameras and IMacs and such
so I can post on the internet
a record of most of my antics.

Now that I'm old I write poems
and I read them in public, to people
who could be my grandchildren
but wouldn't like to be. (It's mutual)